FAIRY TALE COLLECTION

CINDERELLA

RETOLD BY NADIA HIGGINS
ILLUSTRATED BY KATHLEEN PETELINSEK

Published by The Child's World®
1980 Lookout Drive • Mankato, MN 56003-1705
800-599-READ • www.childsworld.com

Acknowledgments
The Child's World®: Mary Berendes, Publishing Director
Red Line Editorial: Editorial direction
The Design Lab: Design, production, and illustration

ISBN 978-1623236083
LCCN 2013931776

Printed in the United States of America
Mankato, MN
July, 2013
PA02179

Long ago, there lived a most unfortunate girl. For though she possessed great beauty and many talents, she lacked love.

The girl's kind mother had been her only friend in the world. But after her mother died, her father married again. His new wife was a most cruel woman, as were her two daughters. The wicked trio took over the girl's home completely. They forced the poor girl to wear tattered rags and to sleep in the kitchen. She also had to take care of the lowliest household chores.

"Wash the staircase!"

"Dust the lights!"

"Scrub the chamber pots!" her tormenters yelled.

The girl did her tasks without complaint. In the evening, she warmed herself by the cinders of the dying fire.

The sisters laughed at the poor girl's sooty skirts, dirtied from the cinders. "Cinderella!

Cinderella!" they teased her. Before long, her own name was quite forgotten.

Cinderella's father did nothing to protect his daughter from this treatment. Was he weak or just cold-hearted? We shall never know.

One day, news arrived that the prince was going to give a ball at the palace.

All the fashionable young women were invited. This included the stepsisters, but not Cinderella. Cinderella's stepsisters flew into a tizzy, acting snobbish and important for having been invited.

For days, Cinderella polished and sewed and braided and pinned. She helped the sisters try out every kind of dress and hairdo. Still, they could not decide. In their hearts, they knew that Cinderella had far better taste than they. In desperation, they asked Cinderella for her opinion.

Did she give a false answer? No, Cinderella was too kind to do that. She gave them her best advice.

That evening, the sisters left for the ball looking their very finest. Cinderella stood watching their carriage roll away.

Plop. Plop. Splat! Alone at last, Cinderella let her tears flow freely. Oh, why was her life so wretched?

"Don't cry, my dear child."

"Who's there?" Cinderella startled at the unfamiliar voice.

"It is I, your fairy godmother." An old, hunched-over woman had magically appeared and stepped into view. A smile pulled back the curtains of her wrinkled face. "I've come to prepare you for the ball," she said, holding up a magic wand.

Cinderella only stared, but the fairy godmother put her to work. First, she asked

Cinderella to fetch the largest pumpkin from the garden. The fairy godmother tapped the pumpkin with her wand and—*poof!* It turned into a golden coach.

Next, Cinderella hurried to bring the mousetrap from the kitchen as requested. She lifted the trap door and—*poof!* Six squeaky mice became six snorting horses to pull the coach.

Poof! A plump rat became a stout coachman to drive the horses. And—*poof!* A lizard turned into a fine footman to open the carriage door.

The fairy godmother nodded at her good work. "That should do it." She looked at Cinderella, who shyly hung her head. "Aren't you pleased, my dear?"

"Oh, yes!" Cinderella looked up. "It's only that my clothes—"

"Of course!" *Poof!* In an instant, Cinderella's dirty rags vanished and she was twirling in a gown of golden cloth. Glass slippers seemed to wrap her tiny feet in shimmery moonlight.

As Cinderella climbed into the coach, her godmother shouted a warning. "Come back by twelve o' clock! At midnight's final chime, the spell will be broken. All will be as it was before!"

"I will! . . . And, thank you!" Cinderella called as the carriage rumbled away.

Did the prince really gasp when Cinderella entered the ballroom? He did, and many heard him. For as Cinderella made her entrance, the violins stopped playing, and a hush fell across the ballroom. After a moment, whispers rippled through the crowd. Everyone imagined she was a princess.

That night, the prince rarely left Cinderella's side. She and the prince danced and laughed and talked the night away.

"Who *is* that lovely princess?" everyone wondered. Cinderella's stepsisters didn't even recognize her.

As for Cinderella, she was having such a splendid time that she had quite forgotten her promise to her fairy godmother until—*bong! bong! bong!* The midnight chimes began to ring!

Cinderella leapt to her feet and darted away. "Wait!" the prince called after her. But Cinderella could not even spare the time to turn her head. Panting, she reached the palace gates. As she fled down the stairs, one glass slipper fell off her foot.

"Princess?" The prince called after her, realizing he didn't even know his new love's name. He scanned the palace gardens, but all he saw was a peasant girl running in the distance.

As the prince slowly turned away, a silvery glint caught his eye. "Ho-ho!" He hollered with delight as he picked up Cinderella's dainty glass slipper.

The next day, the entire kingdom buzzed with news from the prince. He announced he would marry the girl whose foot fit the slipper!

Looking for a princess, he brought the shoe to every nearby noble home, but found no match. He then determined to personally test every fair foot in the kingdom.

Cinderella could hardly breathe when she heard the prince's caravan arrive outside. She stood silently in the doorway as the royal party swept in. Right away, her stepsisters grabbed for the slipper. What a fuss they made trying to fit their big feet into the tiny shoe!

"It is no use," the prince said, cupping the slipper in his hands.

At that, Cinderella stepped into the room. "May I try?"

"You?" the elder sister snapped, while the other snorted. "The cinder-wench? What a joke!"

But the prince had already recognized his love's kind eyes. He took Cinderella by the hand and seated her beside him. He slipped the shoe on. Of course, it fit perfectly.

So astonished were the stepsisters, their mouths hung open like barn doors.

They sputtered and gasped as Cinderella pulled the other slipper from her pocket. "A perfect match," the prince said, smiling.

Indeed, they were—Cinderella and the prince, that is. For the happy couple was soon married. As for Cinderella's stepmother and stepsisters, they promised to mend their wicked ways. And Cinderella's father apologized for failing to stop their cruelty.

The new princess gladly forgave them. She invited them to live with her in the palace. And so it was that a most unfortunate girl came to live happily ever after.

FAIRY TALES

Cinderella's story began in someone's imagination. *Whose* imagination exactly, we will never know. This tale can be traced back more than a thousand years to ancient China. Other versions of the story come from many other countries, including Greece, Italy, and Egypt.

For hundreds of years, the story was told and remembered. It wasn't read out of a book. It wasn't considered a children's story, either. Whole families would delight in the details of those wicked sisters and that handsome prince. No doubt, storytellers made up new twists to spice things up!

In 1697, a Frenchman named Charles Perrault published a version of "Cinderella" that became very popular. The story you just read is faithful to his version. More than one hundred years later, Jacob and Wilhelm Grimm of Germany, better known as the Brothers Grimm, published another famous account. In this one, Cinderella's stepsisters get their eyes pecked out by birds!

Cinderella's story wasn't told only for entertainment. Like many tales, it was meant to teach important lessons about how to live. Cinderella is rewarded for being sweet and kind. *Be good* is certainly one moral of this story. Another message is that love can turn up when someone least expects it. Or that no one is alone, even when it feels that way.

What if you could write your own version of Cinderella's story? What details would you add or change? What lessons would your story teach?

ABOUT THE AUTHOR

Nadia Higgins is the author of more than sixty books for children. She lives in Minneapolis, Minnesota, with her husband and two daughters.

ABOUT THE ILLUSTRATOR

Kathleen Petelinsek loves to draw and paint. She lives next to a lake in southern Minnesota with her husband, Dale; two daughters, Leah and Anna; two dogs, Gary and Rex; and her fluffy cat, Emma.